THE NATURALIST BEAUTY
BRYANT QUIOVERS

THE NATURALIST BEAUTY

THE NATURALIST BEAUTY

BRYANT QUIOVERS

Lulu.com
2019

ACKNOWLEDGEMENT

Many thanks to my loyal readers. I enjoy creating the fantasy for you.

CHAPTER ONE

The lights flickered inside Jordan Fallon's five bedroom Cameron Lake Community home as lightning lit up the evening sky. The heavy wind and rain crashed against the windows and the freshly planted trees swayed back and forth on the manicured lawn. Thunder storms were a normal occurrence in costal areas but that was no peace of mind for home owners. He would have to call the landscapers out again.

Jordan was just glad that he had finish cooking his favorite meal, shrimp fettuccine Alfredo. He always made way more than he could eat, so he could share and boast about his cooking. He topped his meal off with a large glass of sweet red wine, which his doctor suggested do to his middle age.

A single place setting at an eight seat formal dining table may seem pretentious to most people, but not for

Jordan Fallon. He loved the large spaces he created for himself. His five bedrooms, three and a-half bath with a double garage and kidney shape pool was his sanctuary. He did not entertain guess save the weekly housekeeper and landscapers. Not many people even knew what side of town he lived on, not even his family.

The sound of the doorbell was so strange that it took a few rings for Jordan to realize what it was. He certainly wasn't expecting guests, but with the weather being so horrific it must be some sort of emergency. He hadn't taken a bite of his fettuccine. He took a sip of wine then went to answer the door.

"Shana!" Jordan exclaimed seeing the tiny brown eyes peeking from under the sopping wet woolly afro.

Shana clung to herself soaking wet down to her flat thong sandals. Her spaghetti strap top and full length skirt dripped water on the stoop. Her phone was the only thing that didn't get wet locked away in a zip lock bag. She thought she had gotten the wrong address.

"Get it here," Jordan grabbed Shana's boney arm and pulled her into the foyer and closed the heavy door. "You are soaked," he said overstating the obvious leading her to the guest bathroom.

Shana looked around at all of the framed paintings on the walls, the large chandelier hanging from the vaulted ceiling, the polished winding staircase and floors. The bathroom was nearly twice the size of her bedroom.

"Take off those wet things," he said handing her a big white terry-cloth bathrobe and slippers. "I will wash them for you. Come to the dining room once you have changed."

Shana felt as stupid as looked to herself in the full-length mirror. She slid the skirt off which dragged the ground heavy from the rain. Her top was also heavy from the rain. She dried her smooth brown skin and fluffed her bush then put on the soft bathrobe. She fluffed her afro with the towel drying it the best she could. Some how her reflection looked different wrapped in the fine robe and house slippers. Everything looked so sparkling clean. Her own clothes looked as if they had been found in a dumpster.

"Come and sit," Jordan said taking the wet clothes and sandals wrapped in a towel when Shana came to the dining room. "I'll take those. I was just sitting down to eat."

"I'm sorry. I didn't mean..."

"None sense, you didn't come all this way in the rain for nothing," Jordan said taking the wet clothes to the laundry room behind the kitchen. "I set a place for you. It's one of my favorites, shrimp fettuccine alfredo. I add a few extra vegetables to give it my own flavor." He poured the large Bordeaux half full for her. "It's a sweet red. Good for your heart. At least that's what my doctor says," he chuckled taking a sip of the wine.

Shana followed his example sipping from the large glass.

"I think this is the best I every made," Jordan moaned as he chewed the food.

Shana nodded in agreement. She was hungrier than she thought. She could taste all of the main ingredients on her pallet. She surprised herself with her smile. It had been a dreadful day.

"So, how did you find out where I live?" he asked watching her closely to see if she was going to get creative.

"I got it off a shipping package you gave Aunt Becky," she replied without hesitation.

"Would you like some more," he said taking up her plate without waiting on her answer.

"Do you live here alone?" Shana asked.

"Yes. I figured out that I am not good at being in a relationship and I love the freedoms that comes with living by myself," he return the plate with more food on it. "No dogs, cats, birds and not even goldfish."

Shana chuckled. She did not like being in a relationship either. "Yeah, I'm not dating either," she agreed.

"Why not, you're young. You should be trying different things to see what you like," Jordan smiled.

"How did that workout for you?" she replied.

"Rough," he acknowledged.

"This is really good," Shana said finishing the second plate of food. She was full and comfortable in the big soft robe. "This place looks like a show room in a store."

"Thanks. I decorated it myself," he said figuring that she wouldn't know the difference. "Grab your glass." He took up their plates and headed to the kitchen. He waited until she finished her wine before taking the glass from her. "You can take a look around while I finish the dishes."

"I hope that I don't get lost," Shana chuckled feeling a slight buzz from the wine.

She was curious to see the rest of the house. It barely looked lived in, more like rooms in a hotel. Each bedroom she entered was decorated differently but with a common color scheme from accented walls to heavy wood molding. The furniture and drapes looked very expensive. She guided her fingers over the surfaces, but was careful not to touch anything.

The master bathroom looked more like a spa done in beige and brown, marble walls and floor, walk-in glass front shower with double ceiling heads. It also had a step-up garden whirlpool bathtub.

"Go ahead and try it," Jordan said leaning against the bathroom door frame holding an opened bottle of champagne and two flutes. He had changed his shirt for a smoking jacket and glasses in place of his contacts.

Charismatic grown man Shana thought seeing how classic he appeared though she doubted he'd smoke a cigar. Sitting on the edge of the tub naked under the terry-cloth robe she assessed the scene to be very romantic. She turned on the water in the tub subtly agreeing to play her part.

"Bubbles," he handed her a glass of champagne.

"Thank you," she softened her tone.

"I usually don't invite people into my home, but I am glad that you are here and I am enjoying your company," he said looking deep into her eyes as if he could touch her soul.

"You came to mind and the next thing I knew, I was on the bus," Shana sipped the champagne feeling her heart beat in her ears. "When I saw the house, I thought I gotten the address wrong. It doesn't look like you live alone. All the rooms have beds and dressers in them."

"Why have rooms with nothing in them?" he smiled.

She knew from the look in his eyes that they were going to have sex. Why hadn't she shaved her pubic hair? She haven't been very active since she began going natural. She had actually made out with more girls than guys in recent months. She knew that she was going to see a man at his home in the evening, not just any man. An old school player.

"I've been admiring your natural look. I find a natural woman to be stunning and you have captivated me many times," he said refilling her glass.

Shana was still looking into his eyes and it seemed as if his voice was inside of her head. She could hear his words, but his lips didn't seem to be moving. His lips looked soft and moist to her. His lips were so close to hers. He was whispering. His lips were against hers. Did she kiss him or did he kiss her. She didn't know.

Jordan held her with his hand to the side of her neck kissing her gently, savoring the softness of her lips. His cock strained and jerked in his pants, and then there was the gentle touch of her hand on her hardon.

Shana stroked then length of his long thick dick through his pants. She felt it jerk under her touch. She like that bit of control. Boys usually bend to her will when she held their cocks in her hand. It's length excited her. With her touch, she imagined it to be unbelievably huge. She became more curious by the second to see it.

Jordan broke their kiss slowly then stood. Shana looked up at him while he removed his robe. His body was firm, muscular and hairless. She hadn't imagined him at all. He had been this old guy that flirted with her aunt. She didn't wonder how big and hard his dick would be. She did not contemplate having him on top of her or her being on top of him. He was just a kinda cool old man that her aunt called when she needed a favor. She was now imagining his cock as he unfastened his pants.

Jordan stepped out of his shoes before opening his pants to reveal his massive hardon. He pushed down his pants and his big black dick sprung up like a jack-in-a-box.

"It's huge!" Shana exclaimed catching the long thick shaft with both hands. She inspected the circumcised then took it into her mouth. Her soft lips slid from the rim to the tip with a smack. "Mmmm," she moaned sliding the helmet shaped head in and out of her wet mouth. She stroked the thick cock with the same motion she took it into her mouth. She slid her lips down the underside of the long pole and sucked on each of his balls.

"That's real good," Jordan complemented her skills.

Shana showed that she really liked sucking cock stuffing the head into her throat. "I'm good at a few things," she replied. She cradled his ballsack in one hand and stroked his length with the other licking up and down the shaft.

Jordan brought her to her feet and removed her robe. His eyes fell down over her up turned breasts, across her rippled stomach to her hairy bush then back to her brown eyes. "You are so fine," he said guiding her down on the thick floor mat.

"Ugh!" Shana groan receiving the first hard thrust from Jordan. "Ugh! Ugh! Ugh! Please! Please!" she strained holding her hand to block his hips from sending such a power blow. "Softer please," she complained holding her hand against his chest. "You are too big for me. It hurts. Your dick is really big."

"Oh I'm sorry," he whispered pushing her calves to his neck and sliding his hands under her shoulders hooking her into a ball under him. He pushed his rock hard cock as deep as her could and began to grind. "Is that better."

Shana closed her eyes as the big black monster cock stretched her insides. The pleasure was matching the pain and she did not know which way to lean. It took a few minutes before the pleasure to win out with him pounding her tight pussy again. His lips at her neck whispering beautiful words increased the intensity of the sensation she was beginning to feel. Her toes tingled. She dug her fingernails into his skin as she strained.

"Grrraaah!" Jordan growled shooting his thick cum into the young woman's tight pussy. He slowed his stroke and released her legs.

Shana smiled brightly looking up into his almond shaped brown eyes. She understood what she had felt to be an orgasm. It definitely lived up to the hype.

"Oh, you like that huh?" Jordan chuckled slowly pulling out of her.

Shana giggled.

"How about we get these jets going," he said pressing the chrome button on top of the tub. He filled her glass with champagne once she was seated in the warm water.

"This is nice," she said looking around the bathroom sipping from the flute. Her pussy ached, but she was liking the feeling.

"Thank you, and I hope that you will allow me to shave that big bush," he replied slowly.

Shana nodded in spite of her insecurities about it. She had only been fucked by boys, never a man. She had seen men dicks before, but none the size of Jordan's. The only guy that she knew that had a dick as big as Jordan's huge cock was her cousin Nick. She had never sucked or held Nick's cock, but from what she saw it was plenty big.

Jordan put her legs over his and pulled her on his lap. "Your Aunt would shit bricks if she found out about what we are doing," he said sliding her against the underside of his hardening dick.

"I guess we shouldn't tell her then, huh?" Shana mused as he sucked on her brown nipple.

"I was hoping that you would say that," he said licking at her other nipple. "I'm going to take you shopping after we have breakfast in the morning. I really like your style. I think you will like this shop I saw. They carry that earthy-hippie look."

"Bohemian Boutique?" she ask raising so that the monster cock could slid back into her aching pussy. She strained as she came down on the long thick pole.

"Yes, that's it. Bohemian Boutique. Have you been there before?" he asked not forcing himself in her.

"Couldn't afford too," she moaned seating herself firmly. She felt stuffed with him but wanted that feeling back more. She began rotating her hips.

"I will go with you tomorrow so you can afford some things," Jordan said grinding with her. "I really like your boobs." He massaged the ripe tits. "I'm glad that you found me."

"Mmmm," Shana moaned as her orgasm built. She rocked back and forth faster and faster as the sensation grew. "Uuuugh!" Her entire body shivered.

Jordan was primed and ready. His dick was so hard that its head was painful. He wanted her in a more comfortable spot to do her how he really wanted to. He slid out of her pushing her back so that her tits floated with the bubbles. "Time for a quick clean shave," he said getting out of the tub.

Shana was still basking in the glow of her orgasm until Jordan returned with clippers, a towel and his shaving kit.

"You're really going to like the feel of being really smooth down there," he said helping her to sit on the towel straddling the tub. He wasted no time knocking off the hairy bush but being careful to go in the direction of the growth of her hair.

Shana watched curiously sipping on another glass of champagne. She had shaved her bikini line, but had never cut it all off. She was proud of it when it had begun to grow. It had made her feel more mature. No boy had ever complained about it. Though none of them had ever attempted to go down on her as other girls spoke of. Jordan was no boy. He covered her entire crotch and way up between the crack of her ass with the shaving cream. With smooth strokes he took the hair away leaving only the smooth skin.

"Absolutely amazing," Jordan said wiping away the remains of the shaving cream. "Now I can enjoy kissing those lips also." He helped her all the way out of the tub and took her directly to his bed.

With a swing of his hand, Jordan turned down the covers on his big California king sized bed. Shana felt light as a feather as he lifted her on it. He was clearly in control placing her how he wanted her to be on the bed.

"Aaaahhh!" Shana moaned. The feel of his lips and tongue on her freshly shaved cunt was like rumbling ice on her nipples. It sent shock waves from her toes to the top of her head.

Jordan had years of practice at cunnilingus and he relished the opportunities to show off his pussy eating skills every chance he got. He counted a score every time she came under the power of his greedy mouth.

"I don't think I can take anymore," Shana pleaded.

Jordan raised pulling her under him and pinning her knees to her shoulders as he guided his rock hard monster cock inside of her pretty brown pussy. He grunted as he slammed into her. He was relentless driving his cock with all his might. He blocked out everything in his mind. He was starting to believe that she was the young woman that he wanted. The woman that he had fantasized about possessing mind, body and soul. First he would have to make her desire him. He would have to turn her completely out.

Shana was caught in a state of perpetual orgasmic bliss. Her vagina felt as it had been pounded and molded to the shape of his huge circumcised cock. Being turned onto her knees and having her ass pounded against the headboard, her aching rectum was the blazing tale-tale sign of her long night of getting her brains fucked out.

CHAPTER TWO

"What is this, the MILF club," Nick chuckled entering the living room seeing his mother and her lady friends in their short sun dresses sipping on mimosas.

The ladies giggled embracing the compliment from the young Nubian who filled the room with his presence. Willow and Marie crossed their legs feeling the young man's eyes burning the insides of their thighs. Rachel squeezed her thighs and her large tits together bashfully. Becky giggled seeing the ladies ogle her handsome son.

"You are so gorgeous," Nick leaned over giving his mother a kiss on the cheek.

"Awww, that is so sweet," Marie muse lifting her open cleavage higher.

"Have you seen Shana," Becky asked.

"Not since yesterday," Nick said taking a sip of his mother's drink. "I'm pretty sure she's fine where ever she is. She knows how to take care of herself."

"What have you been up to today?" Willow batted her long eye lashes.

"Helping Rico with Riley's birthday present," Nick winked at Rachel.

"What did he get her?" Rachel asked.

"I'm not telling. It's a secret," Nick laughed giving Becky another kiss and headed off to his bedroom.

"They are so damn secretive about everything," Willow said finishing her drink. "I know how to get it out of him." She stood straightening her dress then strutted after Nick.

"Girl, you better leave that boy alone," Becky chuckled.

"I got this," Willow waved them off.

"Girl, that boy of yours is so fine," Marie said.

"Trust me, he knows it," Becky laughed.

"I never know what to get Riley," Rachel said. "Rico has always picked out her gifts and she always loved them."

"Shit, they've been together since grade school haven't they?" Marie asked.

"Yep," Becky replied. "Nicholas, Rico, Riley and Shana all went to school together and Rico has been with her everyday since, right?"

"Yep, some days I wake up not knowing if she's at home or over at his house," Rachel said. "She loves the shit out of that boy."

"I don't know what Willow is thinking, but there is no way Nicholas would ever tell a secret," Becky said.

"I'm sorry honey, but he could damn sure keep a secret with me if he wanted," Marie said giving one of her big tits a firm squeeze.

"Josh not giving it to you?" Becky joked.

"Not as well as I think Nicholas could," Marie laughed.

"Yeah honey, I've been tempted more than a few times. The way he looks at you, you can see the desire," Rachel said squeezing both of her tits together.

"Y'all are playing but that boy only got two things on his mind and the other one is money," Becky chuckled.

Their conversation was interrupted by Willow's cries of pleasure echoing through the house. The three ladies laughed hysterically.

"OH! OH! OH!" Willow cried out.

Several minutes later, they ladies listened more intently.

"Yes! Please! Oh! Fuck yeah! Oh shit!" Willow cried out.

"Damn, he is really giving it to her," Marie said.

"I told you," Becky chuckled.

"And he'll keep a secret?" Rachel asked listening as best she could to what was going on in Nick's bedroom.

"Honey, he'll only tell what you absolutely need to know," Becky confirmed.

"Shit! He's doing her an awfully long time," Marie said. "It's been almost a half hour." She made another drink and drunk it fast. "I'm going to need something harder than this."

Becky chuckled going to the kitchen while the other two ladies strained to hear the fucking going on in the house.

Rachel followed by Marie joined Becky in the kitchen so they could hear better. Becky poured them shots of brandy. Willow's screams shook them. They were both excited and a little scared.

"SHIT! I'M CUMMING!" Willow screamed.

The three ladies finished their drink and got another. They listened to the shower going in the bathroom and then a little while later Nick came to the kitchen with a towel wrapped around his waste.

"Okay, you next," Nick said taking Rachel's wrist and pulling her behind him.

Rachel look to Becky and Marie asking what she should do.

"Go on girl," Marie said. "Hell, you need it badder than any of us."

Nick pulled Rachel into his bedroom closing his door behind them. He grabbed her slamming her body against his. "I knew one day I would have a shot at you," he said taking the back of her neck then forcing her into a hard kiss.

"Can you tell me what Rico is getting Riley for a birthday present?" Rachel asked allowing Nick to free her large melons from her dress.

"These are the reason I like coming over to your house," Nick said lifting the heavy tits. "They are not only huge, but they are swollen and beautiful too." He sucked hard on one of the erect nipples then the other. He kissed and licked them, putting his face between them.

"Just wanted to be sure that I didn't get the same gift that Rico got for her," Rachel said as he removed her dress.

"Don't worry, you didn't get her the same gift that he got for her," Nick said moving her over to the bed.

"I got her a present and I didn't want to get her the same thing," she said as he laid down.

"It's a secret," Nick smiled pushing her legs up and spreading them wide. "I promise you didn't get her the same thing."

"How do you know?" Rachel said holding her knees up to her shoulders for him.

"What did you get her?" Nick asked giving her a long lick from her asshole to her clit.

"That new cell phone she wanted," Rachel moaned.

"Mmmm," Nick moaned sucking on Rachel's clit. "Lady cock." He teased the large clit with the tip of his tongue.

Rachel smashed his face down on her nob as she began to cum. She masturbated often being able to bring herself off almost anywhere including in her car and her desk at work. It didn't take very much manipulation of her clit to set her off.

"Oh yeah!" Nick groaned pulling her to the edge of the bed and pushing her legs back up. He drilled his big black dick into her wet pussy with a single stroke. He held her thighs as he pounded her with all his might.

Rachel moaned uncontrollably. He had her in the perfect spot and he was hitting it hard. She could hardly believe her own begging and pleading. His cock felt so big stretching her greedy cunt.

Nick nearly forgot the time. His dick felt as hard as steel and he did not want to stop pounding Rachel's pretty cunt, but he purposely saved Marie for last. He also needed to get ready for Riley's party.

"I'd like to hit this on a regular," Nick said slowing his stroke.

"I'd really like that," Rachel replied trying to calm herself down. "I still would like to know what Rico is getting Riley for her birthday."

"It's huge, but I can't tell anyone," Nick said slowing sliding his rock hard cock out of her pussy. "You'll going to love what he got her. I'm proud of my boy for always treating her so well."

"Me too," Rachel said struggling to stand. "There's no doubt how much he loves her and she loves him."

"I can hardly wait to get a hold of you again," Nick said pulling her into a hard kiss. He squeezed her large tits before releasing her.

Marie's hands were shaking. She had been playfully teasing Nick for years. He was a grown man now and her fear was that she might not measure up to all the boasting she had done at his expense. She avoided Becky's eyes and Willow was still moaning over her sore vagina. Rachel looked as if she had been in a jungle fight.

Nick charged into the kitchen and swept Marie into his strong arms and whisked her away to his bedroom.

"OH! OH FUCK!" Marie's cries echoed throughout the house.

"I told Marie that she had better stop messing with that boy," Becky laughed.

"Did he tell you what Rico got Riley for her birthday?" Willow asked Rachel.

"No, but he definitely knows how to through that dick down," Rachel chuckled through clinched lips.

"Okay, don't none of you bitches get any ideas about trying to lock baby down," Becky said. "He's way too young for that."

"I think you got that in reverse," Willow laughed squeezing her thighs together.

"AAAAHHH!" Marie screamed.

"He really knows how to dick a bitch down," Rachel laughed.

The ladies put themselves back together while listening to Marie's cries of pleasure. Nick was giving Marie the fucking of her life. Even Becky became a little worried about her friend. Nick's head board sounded like hammering against the wall.

All of the noise stopped abruptly. The ladies stopped what they were doing to listen to what was coming next. There were sounds of a door closing then the sound of the shower in the bathroom.

Willow looked at her watch and nodded clearly impressed. The other ladies agreed. A little while later Marie came down the hall with her curly locks still damp from the shower. The ladies stared at her waiting to here what happened.

"What?" Marie smirked.

"You know what," Becky said.

"Dish bitch," Willow agreed.

"He went all the way down through there, front and back," Marie blushed to the ladies amusement. "I can't remember getting it so good and like forever."

The ladies laughed hysterically.

Nicholas finally came out in white linens and sandals. He always dressed dapper, mature beyond his years. His white fedora gave him an even more sophisticated look. "Ladies, it has been a pleasure, but I have to run," he said with a slight smile. "Thanks mom. I love you," he whispered in Becky's ear while giving her a hug. "Take a car. None of y'all are any shape to be driving. I'll text you the address to the party mom."

CHAPTER THREE

Riley giggled joyfully holding on to Rico's lean but muscular arm. Cars were parked all the way down the street in both direction. The three bedroom renovated historic house with the white picket fence were packed with seemingly everyone Riley had known during her lifetime. Presents were staked high in the dining room and a three foot tall birthday cake sat on top of the table. The food was setup on tables in the cute little well manicured back yard which held a double car garage with barn doors.

"This is a really great party," Heidi, one of Riley's old classmates said bouncing out to the dance area in the back yard.

"How did you find all of these people?" Riley asked Rico. "That's Alexis West!"

"Most of them were on social media," Rico chuckled. "You are so adorable, everyone wants to be apart of your life."

"As long as I have you, the rest is just frosting," she turned kissing his soft lips for what have been the millionth time.

"Okay, everyone inside. It's time to cut this big ass cake," Rico announced.

Shana stood next to Riley and Nicholas bought in a stool for Riley to stand on. Everyone jammed in shoulder to shoulder as Rico lit the candles on the cake.

"Happy birthday too you," Shana began to sing being joined by everyone else.

Everyone cheered and applauded after Riley blew out the candles.

"What did you wish for?" someone asked.

"I already have my wish," Riley replied leaning down to kiss Rico to everyone's amusement. She reached out to Nicholas giving him a soft kiss at the corner of his mouth then gave Shana a lingering hug.

Rico knelt at the stool Riley stool upon and held up an engagement ring in a black box. The party goers got even loader and Riley screamed to the top of her lungs.

"YES! YES! YES!" Riley screamed though no one really heard the question.

The music was turned up a little louder. A little more alcohol was spilled and people held each other a little tighter.

Rico wrapped his arms around Riley from behind. "Time for you to unwrap my present," he whispered in her ear and kissed her neck.

"Hey cousin, I heard that you took on the four Gypsies today," Shana mused taking hold of Nicholas' arm to follow Rico and Riley to the garage.

"Yes, it was lots of fun," Nick chuckled.

"Must have been, they can't seem to stop talking about it," Shana giggled.

"Have I finally peeked your interest?" Nick teased.

"I've always been interested, just didn't know if you could handle me or not," Shana laughed.

"Oh, you can bet your sweet brown ass I can handle it," Nick responded.

"We'll just have to find out then, one of these days," Shana teased.

"Close your eyes and no peaking," Rico told Riley and nodded to Nicholas and Shana to open the garage doors.

The crowd gasped seeing the mariner color European convertible sports coupe. Riley was speechless guiding her trembling fingers along the shiny paint and tanned leather interior.

"I told you he didn't get her the same thing as you," Nick said nudging Rachel who made her way through the crowd to get a better look.

"This is the best birthday ever," Riley said reaching out for Rico with tears of joy filling her eyes.

"He really went all out, didn't he?" Rachel said.

"You don't know the half of it yet," Nicholas replied.

"Remember all of the plans and dreams we shared?" Rico began. "I want to start living them now."

Riley flashed her steel blue eyes up at him.

"You said that you wanted small house with a white picked fence and colorfully decorated," Nicholas said.

Riley looked back at the cute little historical house.

"I want to marry you right here, next Saturday in our house," Rico concluded.

"Our house?" Riley asked in near disbelief.

"Nicholas helped me with a lot of things, but yes, our house," Rico said with his hands firmly planted on her hips. "I've been in love with you since the first time we played in the sand together at the beach. You are as much apart of me as the wind and the air. You make me happy."

"And you make me happy. Yes, we can marry on Saturday," Riley replied kissing her husband to be.

"You heard it," Nick announced. "We have a wedding right here next Saturday. Do not leave without your invitations."

"You had wedding invitations made already?" Rachel asked.

Rico smiled.

"Planned every detail," Shana giggled giving Riley a hug. "Now, lets go take a look at your wedding dress. It's upstairs in your attic."

Rico was pulled into the crowd with Nick by his side being congratulated.

"Wedding dress? I can't believe he done all of this without at least consulting me," Rachel whispered to Becky.

"Why not?" Becky asked as they made their way into the house behind Riley and Shana. "Whenever it comes to Riley, Rico does exactly what he want, and Nicholas is going to make sure of it."

"But her wedding dress," Rachel pleaded. "I thought that would be something that she and I would do together, and make plans for her wedding."

"Riley has been planning her wedding to Rico since they were children," Becky laughed. "Just remember dear, this is about Riley not you."

"You're right," Rachel hugged Becky as they entered the attic behind Riley and Shana.

Willow and Marie entered the attic as stunned as everyone else. The wedding dress stood on a mannequin next to the window lit by the full moon. The white sheer and lace off the shoulder gown with a long train was stunning. There were quiet cooing among the ladies.

"What about the fit?" Rachel asked. "You have to have a fitting."

"Rico was very careful about that," Shana said.

Riley pushed her long skirt down to her sandals and pulled her cropped top off over her head freeing her naked boobs. Shana smiled at how comfortable her friend always seemed to be naked in front of people.

"This is the exact dress that I wanted," Riley said pulling it off the mannequin.

Becky nudged Rachel.

"It's gorgeous sweetheart," Rachel said coming to help Riley with the dress.

The dress was a perfect fit with a length to match her bare feet. The lace silhouetted her breast crotch and the crack of her ass allowing the sheer to show off the rest of her figure.

"Perfect for a virgin bride," Shana said.

"Virgin?" Rachel questioned.

The ladies giggled.

"Yes I'm a virgin mother," Riley replied.

"But I saw you naked in bed with him," Rachel said.

"Yes, mother we have been naked together, made out and even slept together, but we never had intercourse," Riley said. "We decided a long time ago that we would have some experiences but would save that for our wedding night."

"That is extraordinarily wonderful my dear," Becky said.

"Yes, give me five minutes with that stud and my panties would be down around my ankles," Willow joked.

"You don't wear panties," Marie added to the others amusement.

"Well, what about shoes?" Rachel asked.

"White laced flats. Rico said never any heels, wedges are okay, but she much rather wear flats," Shana said handing a shoe box to Rachel.

Riley giggled recalling words she had spoke to Rico.

"Oh, and this," Shana revealed a jewelry box with a coin in it. "Nicholas found this. He said it would be something maybe too hard to find. It's a sixpence. I never knew such a thing."

"Something old, something new, something borrowed and something blue. A sixpence in your shoe," Willow said. "Four good luck pieces plus a sixpence to bring prosperity."

"That is so wonderful," Becky smiled.

"Something borrowed," Rachel said removing her diamond tennis bracelet. "Of all the things I possess this is the most precious to me besides you."

"Something new," Willow removed her new diamond earrings and handed them to Riley.

"I got something blue," Shana pulled up her dress to remove her Sapphire belly button ring.

"Do anyone wear panties anymore more," Marie chuckled.

"Only when necessary dear," Becky mused.

"I have the best friend in the world," Riley pulled Shana into a deep passionate kiss to the cheers of the ladies. "Thank you all so very much."

"Does that mean that Rico is a virgin too?" Willow asked.

"We haven't gone all the way, but trust me. He knows exactly what to do with that big cock of his," Riley laughed. "We have waited for this for what seems like forever. It's perfect." She hugged Shana tightly.

"What about your hair?" Rachel asked. "I can bread it for you, if you like and do a light makeup." Her tone was clearly pleading.

"Yes, of course mother. You can do my hair," Riley smiled.

"Thank you so much sweetheart," Rachel hugged her.

"No, thank you mother," Riley kissed her mother's cheek.

"Invitations," Marie said taking a card out of the box. "This box is post marked two months ago. He's planned this up to the day?"

"Well, more like a year and a half," Shana said. "It took Rico a while to find this house, get every room painted and the furniture that he knew Riley would like."

Riley giggled squeezing Shana again.

"Come on, lets get you out of that dress before you wrinkle it," Becky said.

"I love all of it," Riley said.

The party continued until just before midnight leaving Nicholas, Shana, Riley and Rico to clean up the mess.

"I could not have done this without the two of you," Rico said.

"That's right, you couldn't have," Nick joked.

Shana punched his shoulder.

"You two are the best friends that anyone could ever hope for," Riley said hugging Shana tight. "So, when are the two of you going to sleep together?"

"We are cousins," Shana protested.

Rico and Nick chuckled as if they held a secret.

"I can feel the love between you two," Riley said. "Y'all should totally fuck."

"Riley!?" Shana blushed.

"You really should, that way it would be the four of us together," Riley replied going into the house with Shana.

"Riley Nick don't want to be tied down and neither do I," Shana said. "I love being able to go where I want, hang out with who I and and to have sex with who I want without having to consider anyone else feelings."

"Then just sleep with him," Riley said.

"Are you my pimp, now?" Shana said.

"No," Riley grabbed Shana and pinned her against the wall. "After the wedding I want all of us to live together. We have three bedrooms. You and I make out now, but think how good it would be with the four of us making out together."

"You are planning group sex before your wedding day," Shana mused.

"The wedding is very important to me, but the reality is that he only puts his dick in my pussy," Riley said. "I want our sex life to be free with the people that we care about."

"But you have never made out with anyone beside Rico and me, and Rico has never made out with anyone beside you. How do you know how Rico would react to such a thing?" Shana said.

"Because we talked about it," Riley said. "Rico thinks that you are gorgeous and he would love to have sex with you."

"And Rico is going to be okay with Nick having sex with you?" Shana asked.

"Rico told me a long time ago that Nick wanted to fuck me and you. All we need is for you to agree to it," Riley said rubbing her nose against Shana's. Her hands groped Shana's braless tits. She kissed her once then twice. "Let's share all of our love together."

Shana moaned. Her pussy was still throbbing from the endless fucking she had been getting from Jordan. Her clit was a red hot on button and Riley pressed it. Her dress melted away along with her top. They kissed and groped wildly ending up in one of the bedrooms on top of a pallet framed bed. Shana was careful not to penetrate Riley's vagina as usual. Riley's virginity had become important to her also. Riley's asshole was a different matter. The room filled with moans and their scent.

"Dude, you pull everything off very smoothly," Nicholas congratulated his best friend. "Everybody showed up too."

"I know, right?" Rico chuckled.

"Thinking about that wedding night, huh?" Nick joked.

"Naw, Riley and I are good. I mean, I'm looking forward to popping her cherry, but we have so much awesome sex already that it's going to be like a new position," Rico said. "When Riley told Shana she should give you some, my dick got as hard as you said yours did when you saw Riley naked."

"Damn!" Nick exclaimed.

"Riley said that she's down with fucking you and with me fucking Shana," Rico added.

"Seriously?" Nick said.

"Riley want it to be just the four of us, but I told her that you had a lot going on," Rico said.

"Yeah, but that doesn't mean that the four of us still couldn't be together," Nick reasoned. "Seriously, I think that Shana is more than enough for one person. I could definitely see myself being hooked up with her."

They both paused listening to the girls having sex.

"We can't do anything until after you pop her cherry, right?" Nick said eagerly.

"Her vagina is the only thing we need to leave untouched," Rico said.

"Anal is good?" Nick asked.

"Anal is amazing," Rico laughed. "That's why we don't feel like we are missing much. She cums a lot and she likes her ass ridden hard."

"What are y'all talking about?" Riley smiled coming into the living room completely naked with Shana behind her with a towel wrapped around her torso.

"Fucking you and Shana," Rico chuckled pulling his naked fiance onto his lap and winking an eye at Shana.

"Oh yeah, what did y'all come up with?" Riley said kissing Rico's face and lips.

"We want to do it," Nick said pulling Shana from her chair onto his lap.

"But we are cousins," Shana struggle slightly to adjust the towel.

"That's a weak argument and you know it," Nick said.

"Very weak," Rico agreed smiling brightly.

"We're not talking about you and I getting married," Nick began.

"Yet," Riley interrupted. "We are not talking about y'all getting married yet."

"Just fun when we're together," Nick finished.

"I hope I don't regret this," Shana said grabbing Nick's hardon through his linen pants.

Riley giggled kneeling in front of Rico getting his pants down so that she could get to his big hard cock. Nick slipped out of his clothes with ease and presented his massive dick to Shana.

"Damn bro! I hate to say it, but this is some expensive ass furniture for us to be fucking on like this," Nick said.

"The back bedroom?" Rico suggested.

Riley held on to Rico's hard cock following Shana and Nicholas to the back bedroom. They originally thought of the room as a den or game room. It was larger than a bedroom but too small to be a proper den. Rico and Nick built a California king sized platform pallet bed with crate night stands.

Riley and Shana wasted no time getting the guys cocks in their mouths. They never had group sex but they worked well together getting the guys side by side on the bed and licking and sucking on balls to dick head.

"They both have the same size dick," Shana chuckled waving Nick's cock back and forth.

"Our turn," Rico said getting Riley doggie style.

Shana got in the same position pushing her ass up high. She knew exactly where things was going when she felt Nick's tongue pushing into her asshole. It might have been cause for alarm, but Jordan had rode her asshole as hard as he did her pussy.

"This some hot ass shit!" Rico said sliding his throbbing cock into Riley's anus.

"Shit yea!" Nick said slamming into Shana.

At times they slammed their dicks in cadence and other they seemed to compete to see who could drive their cock the hardest. Nonetheless, the ladies were riding the waves of their orgasms. The guys had a good run before falling on their backs. In a twist, Riley and Shana switched cocks sucking the man poles back to rock hard erections. They mounted the guys and guided the monster cocks up their assholes. Rico and Nicholas fist bumped then began thrusting their dicks up into the gorgeous pair of ladies.

"Shit! This is way too good," Nick said. "Shana, you and I should seriously hookup."

"You mean like date?" Shana moaned riding Rico's big black dick.

"Yeah, like a couple," Nick said.

"Wouldn't that cramp your style?" Shana replied.

"We can workout the details later," Nick said. "What do you say? Be my girl?"

"Yes! She will!" Riley moaned through her orgasm bouncing up and down on Nick's rock hard cock.

"Yes!" Shana cried out as her orgasm broke on Rico's dick.

The guys got the ladies in the buck with legs on their shoulders pounding deep into the ladies assholes and then doggie style again before shooting their heavy loads into Riley and Shana's mouths.

"So, does this mean that we're going to have a double wedding on Saturday?" Riley giggled.

"Saturday is your day sweetheart," Shana said.

"And I want to share it with you," Riley said.

"Everything is already in place," Rico said.

"I don't have a dress," Shana protested.

"Weak argument, remember you looked at the dress you said that you would want if you were getting married," Rico said.

"Shana, will you marry me?" Nicholas said taking off his tribal pinky ring and offering it to her.

"You must really like our ass," Shana chuckled. "Yes, I will marry you."

They all cheered.

"Does this mean that I have to save my pussy for our wedding night," Shana laughed.

"Works for me," Nick chuckled burying his faced against her buttcheeks. He moved around the rim of her brownie before pushing it inside.

"Aww that feels so good," Shana moaned.

"We should spend our wedding night like this," Riley said slowing stroking Rico's cock.

"I'm down with that," Rico replied.

"How about it Shana?" Nick asked.

"I'm in," Shana agreed getting off the bed and shaking her brown round buttcheeks on her way out of the bedroom.

Riley got up to follow Shana getting a playful slap on her asscheek by Rico.

"Man, I did not see this coming," Nick said getting off the bed.

"Riley did," Rico chuckled following Nicholas to get their clothes. "She said that y'all were crazy about each other and that y'all were a lot alike."

"I don't know. I've always admired her naturalist beauty, but she has the kind of free spirit that's hard to define," Nick said stepping into his linen pants.

Rico put on his Bali tribal pants leaving his shirt off for what was sure to be more sex with Riley and Shana. "So, what do you think of Riley?" he asked.

"Dude, much better than I had imagined. Shana too," Nick chuckled.

"Definitely," Rico said. "The more Riley talked about us having sex with Shana, the more I wanted to, but I didn't imagine it being so awesome."

"Seriously, I didn't think that I would want to even date one girl, let alone marry one," Nicholas said.

"My brother," Rico put his hand on Nick's shoulder. "You are going to get laid more not less."

"Can we have some wine?" Riley said to Rico on her way to the master bedroom with Shana.

"Sure thing babe," Rico called back.

"You haven't opened my birthday present," Shana said dragging Riley to the three door grain wood armoire. "Open it."

"Okay," Riley giggled excitedly opening the first two doors.

"It's a good thing that we wear the same sizes," Shana gleamed. "I got all of this for you at Bohemian Boutique."

"Hot shit!" Riley rifled through the clothes, opening the other door and the two drawers at the bottom. "There has to be thousands of dollars worth of clothes in here." She held up a dusty blue calico romper and a Stella dress.

"Yep, nearly five," Shana giggled.

"How did you afford all of this?" Riley said slipping on the blue Stella dress and giving Shana the pink one.

"Mr. Jordan. Turns out that he's very well off and lives in this huge house in Cameron Lake Community," Shana said.

"Wow, where all of those rich people live," Riley replied.

"He said that he don't usually invite people to his house," Shana continued. "I wasn't invited. I kinda just showed up. I didn't realize where his house was until I got there. I thought he was cool and I just wanted to hangout."

"Y'all hooked up?" Riley asked.

"For two days," Shana blushed. "He wants to be my Sugar-daddy."

Riley giggled.

"I know that Nick has his things going on too, like with the Gypsies. I don't want to get in his way of making his moves and Mr. Jordan isn't the only man to want a little of my time," Shana said.

"Nicholas is very open minded," Riley giggled. "Talk to him about it. My mother is one of those Gypsies and they can be very generous, and I'm willing to bet that's one of the reasons he got with them."

"That and he likes to fuck," Shana chuckled.

"Definitely that too," Riley laughed. "Let's share these clothes. It's way too much to me."

"Well, I did get some stuff for me," Shana said hanging the Stella dress back in Riley's armoire. She took Riley into the second bedroom to the pastel pink armoire like the one in Riley's bedroom. "I got the same stuff for the both of us since we kinda have the same taste in clothes." She took out a blue Stella dress like the one Riley had on and put it on."

Riley giggled and hugged Shana. "You are my twin sister and lover," she pushed her tongue into Shana's mouth kissing her hard and passionately.

"Girl, you keep my pussy wet," Shana giggled.

"Let me check," Riley chuckled getting her greedy mouth on Shana's cunt before Shana could brace herself.

Shana moaned cumming hard.

"You're right, your pussy is wet," Riley teased.

"You are the reason I love having sex so much," Shana chuckled.

"Good because I plan on having a lot more sex after our wedding," Riley laughed hooking her arm into Shana's and going in with the guys.

"Damn, y'all are so beautiful!" Nick said reaching for Shana's hand.

Riley leaned into Rico wrapping her arms around his neck giving him soft kisses. "I have an idea," she said. "Why don't we switch partners until the wedding night? To give us a little more to look forward too? I'll hookup with Nick and you hookup with Shana. Give you a chance to miss fucking me."

"Girl, you be coming up with so many crazy ideas," Shana laughed.

"Okay," Rico agreed kissing Riley then releasing her to Nick's grasp. "This is going to be fun."

"And I get to shop for Shana's wedding presents," Riley giggled wrapping her arms around Nicholas' neck.

CHAPTER FOUR

Nicholas woke to Riley sucking on his ballsack and stroking his morning hardon. She had that amazing white girl pretty, natural long curly and thick blonde hair, steel blue eyes, tiny pointed nose, a well defined jaw line and smooth tanned skin. To top things off, she was fit with high lifted nearly D-cup breasts, defined stomach muscles, curvy hips, a round ass with shapely thighs and calves. Her joyful spirit and personality made her even more lovable.

"Good morning," Riley said cheerfully licking the precum from the head of Nick's hard dick.

"Good morning yourself gorgeous," Nick chuckled.

"I figured if you came in my mouth first I could get you hard again then you could fuck my ass really hard before we go. Rico and Shana left earlier. He likes taking me to breakfast on the beach, so I think that's where he is taking Shana. Can I ask you something?"

"Yea, sure," Nick smiled at how much her thoughts flow from one subject to another sometimes.

"Did you like fucking Rachel?" she asked.

"Oh yea, why?" he replied.

"I was thinking that I would like Rico to have sex with her and the other Gypsies," she said. "I'm going to be older one day and I would like for him to see that he would enjoy having sex with me when I get older."

"That's something that you'll never have to worry about with Rico. The sun rises and sets on your ass for him," Nick chuckled causing her to giggle.

"I don't want him to ever feel like that he has missed out on anything waiting on me all these years," Riley said taking the throbbing dick head in her mouth and twisting her hand up and down the shaft.

"Your mom is hot and I'm sure that you're going to be even hotter when you get her age," he replied.

"I want him to have sex with as many girls as you have," Riley said stroking the big black dick faster. "I don't want him to feel caged or restricted."

"What about you?" Nicholas asked. "Don't you want to have sex with different people."

"You," Riley giggled.

Nicholas' body jerked. He grunted grabbing hold of the sheets. He couldn't control himself. The first blast of cum filled Riley's mouth, but she swallowed quick enough to catch the second powerful stream. She gulped down the thick seed without spilling a drop.

"Shit!" Nick exclaimed.

"That was a lot of cum," Riley giggled. She stroked his cock slowly making sure that she got all of his sperm. "Why have you never tried anything with me? Rico told me that you wanted to fuck me. It's not like you haven't had many opportunities."

"Because Rico is my bestfriend and I love you as much as I love him. As much as I've wanted you. I would never treat you like a piece of ass," Nicholas said. "I've joked around with Shana, but I never treated her like she was some cheap piece of ass either."

"And that's why I wanted you to fuck me," Riley laughed. "I love you too." She took his dick into her throat then began sucking and licking on it more vigorously bringing it back to full erection.

Nick groan and moaned. She was an incredible cocksucker beyond a shadow of a doubt. She flipped her hair so that he could watch every movement.

"I really like your dick," Riley giggled moving over on her knees and lifting her asscheeks high for him to enter her from behind.

Nick pushed his hard dick smoothly into Riley's asshole. It was a tight grip but slid easily. He gripped her hips and began pumping. Faster and faster he drove his cock as if it was a machine piston. He thought of all the women that he had been with, he wanted her the most, even more than Shana. She had been that one untouchable thing. She even had pretty feet. Every thought he had came to light. She was as magnificent has he had believed.

"Yes! Fuck me Nick! Fuck my ass!" Riley cried out.

Nicholas pounded her with all his might feeling the pleasure in every stroke. He leaned back watching his dick slid in and out of her tight rectum. He fucked her until he was nearly out of breath and flopped down on the bed.

"Mmmm," Riley moaned sucking on his cock vigorously before mounting him. She rocked back and forth leaning back to make sure that every inch of his big black dick was up her asshole. She rode his cock as hard as he fucked her. "Oh fuck! Oh fuck!" her entire body quivered.

Nick thrust his dick up into her, lifting her up to fall back down into his next thrust.

"Shit! Fuck!" she seemed to be going into convulsions.

Nick rolled her over putting her legs to his shoulders and slammed his aching dick back up her asshole.

"Yes! Yes!" she screamed as her orgasm exploded.

Nick grunted shooting one stream after another flooding her bowels. They both collapsed with his cock still in her asshole.

"Damn, my dick is still hard," Nick said moving it slowly in Riley.

"You are liking ass fucking more and more, huh?" Riley teased squeezing her rectum.

"I'm pretty sure that having a dick in my pussy is going to be better, but I really love having a dick up my ass," she chuckled rolling her hips up so he could bury in cock balls deep.

"Where do we have to go?" Nick asked moving his dick more deliberately.

"Get Shana's wedding dress, shoes and accessories, and shop for her wedding presents," Riley said pulling her knees to her shoulders.

"Yes, shit!" Nick look at the time and started thrusting his dick faster. "We're going to have to go now!" He fucked her as fast as he could racing to his climax before hoping off the blue-eyed blond natural beauty.

Riley didn't doddle seeing that Nick was in a hurry to get to somewhere important. She conditioned her hair and let her natural curls fall where they may. She stepped into a new jumpsuit and slipped on a pair of wedged sandals before adding adding beads and necklaces to complete her outfit.

"I love the way you look stunning in no matter what you put on," Nick complimented her obvious great look.

"Thank you sexy man," Riley giggled as they went out to his Sport-Utility Vehicle. "Would you like me to ride with my tits out?" She popped her ripe tits out the top of her smocked jumpsuit.

"I know Rico is not that liberal," Nick laughed starting the vehicle.

"He can be a little conservative at times, but you're not," Riley laughed removing the straps off her shoulder and pushing the top of the jumpsuit down to her waist freeing her braless tits completely.

"Buckle-up," Nick laughed backing out of the driveway.

"Do you want me to suck your dick while you drive or wait to we get where we are going?" she giggled squeezing his crotch.

"Why couldn't we marry each other?" Nick laughed.

"They do look really good together," Riley chuckled massaging Nick's hardon.

"They are more natural than we are," Nick laughed adjusting himself so that Riley could free his cock.

"Rico loves when I put on my alfro wig and pretend to be Shana," she laughed stroking Nick's big black dick slowly.

"Yep, he wants her as much as I want you," Nick said concentrating more on his driving. "When we talk about fucking girls, we always talk about fucking you and Shana."

"But you were fucking all these other girls," Riley said. "I use to get so jealous sometimes. Shana too, but she tried not to show it. She would always say that y'all are cousins so it was not her business."

"Rico was fucking you as much as I was fucking other girls and Shana was going out with more guys than I went out with girls," Nick defended himself.

"Hold my hair," Riley chuckled leaning over in his lap to take his in her mouth.

"Fuck! You are amazing," Nick held the thick blonde curls in one hand and a tight grip on the steering wheel. He didn't realize that he was driving under the speed limit. He was so relieved to put the vehicle in park in his mother's driveway that he shot his load immediately.

"I'm going to get full off your cum," Riley laughed licking her lips. She continued stroking his dick.

"Looks like your mom is here," Nick said seeing the yellow jeep covered with painted flowers.

"Well I definitely need to have your dick hard before we go in now," Riley joked.

"The thought of you makes my dick hard," Nick mused lifting one of her full tits. "We do have to remember that we have shit to do today."

"We were just talking about y'all," Becky greeted Nick and Riley with cheerful hugs when they entered.

"Good, because we have news," Nick said Becky and Rachel kisses.

"What news?" Becky asked.

"We're going to have a double wedding on Saturday," Riley announced. "Nick and Shana are going to get married with me and Rico."

Becky gasped.

"That's some news," Rachel said clearly surprised wiping a drop of cum from Riley's chin with her finger and tasting it.

Riley giggled.

"I gotta go change," Nicholas walked off.

"Nicholas?" Becky went after him.

"Are you going to tell me what's going on? I'm pretty sure that's cum around your mouth," Rachel said. "I'm not judging, I just want to be apart of your life sweetheart. Where is Rico?"

"Rico is with Shana," Riley said. "We decided that I would be with Nick and Shana would be with Rico until the wedding. That way we could have fun and get a chance to miss each other."

"Are you sure you know what you are doing, because the look you have is a freshly fucked one," Rachel said.

"Yes," Riley giggled. "You know how good Nick is. I can hardly get enough of him."

"Riley!?" Rachel exclaimed. "I thought you were going to be a virgin on your wedding day?"

"I am. I have more places for him to put his dick," Riley laughed.

"Sweetheart, I don't want you to end up getting hurt playing games like this," Rachel said.

"Don't worry mother. We all know what we are doing and what we don't know we will figure out," Riley smiled and kissed her mother's cheek. "After the wedding, would you have sex with Rico? His dick is about the same size as Nick's and Nick said that you were amazing."

"Riley!?" Rachel blushed.

"Nick is very obvious, you can tell that he wants to have you, but Rico is more reserved. I would really love for you to have sex with him," Riley said taking her mother's hand. "Don't you think that Nick and I look good together?"

"You are confusing me," Rachel replied.

"I'm just saying that our personalities are a lot more a like than Rico and I," Riley replied.

Nicholas came out with a suit bag and two suitcases. His Boho style was impeccable. From his soft leather shoes to his fedora he was dressed with class.

"I don't even have to pick out his clothes for him," Riley whispered to her mother. "You are so fine," she said wrapping her arms around Nicholas' neck and tongue kissing him.

Nick slid his hands down to Riley's asscheeks squeezing them firmly and pulling her tightly against him body.

"I'm still not getting this," Becky said. "You and Riley are sleeping together and Rico and Shana are sleeping together."

"Yes!" Riley laughed.

"Y'all are asking for trouble," Becky said.

"So what's going to happen if y'all really start to like each other?" Rachel asked.

"We already do," Nick said. "Rico likes Shana and I like Riley."

"So why aren't you marrying Riley? I use to think that y'all were going to get together. Y'all act the same free loving and pretty," Becky said. "I thought Shana liked girls the way she's always kissing on Riley, and Rico is such a sweetheart, not nearly as wild as you two are."

"Rico does seem like more of big brother," Rachel added.

"Rico has his wild sides too," Nick quickly defended his bestfriend. "He's just more quiet about it. He told me that he wanted to fuck you mom."

Riley burst out into laughter. Even Rachel smirked.

"What I'm saying is that I think you and Riley look better together, that all," Becky said.

"Riley makes anyone look good," Nick said.

"You do a great job of looking good all by yourself," Riley kissing him hungrily again.

"See, that's what I'm talking about," Becky said.

"Rico does look very good with Shana," Riley added.

"Y'all need to really figure out what y'all are doing before somebody gets hurt," Rachel said. "Rico don't have a mother they can run and cry to."

"We got this," Riley smiled boldly grabbing Nick's hardon.

"We got to go," Nick said hugging his mother. "It's going to be fine."

"I love you mother," Riley kissed her mother cheek.

"I can hardly wait to get with you again," Nick said kissing Rachel hard and squeezing one of her braless tits.

Rachel melted into his arms. She was still standing in place when Nick and Riley left out the door.

"That's exactly how I feel all the time with you," Riley said as they loaded up the SUV.

"What?" Nick chuckled.

"Mesmerized," Riley laughed. "I should have worn a dress. Much easier to get out of." She pulled her jumpsuit down around her waist after she got in the vehicle.

"You are perfect they way that you are," Nick smiled getting the SUV moving. "You know they got a point. I would love for Rico to marry Shana and we get married. We are all will still be together, so it wouldn't be that big of a deal, would it?"

"Except for everybody expecting Rico and I to get married and we have been talking about our wedding night for years," Riley said. "I'm really feeling that you and I should get married too."

"No matter what happens, we will all still be together," Nick concluded pulling into an automobile dealership.

"I bet it was your idea to get me a convertible, wasn't it?" Riley said looking at the vast array of sports cars.

"I was thinking that Shana would really love a champagne color convertible like yours for a wedding present," Nick said giving Riley a soft kiss. "We're going to make this quick so we can go get her wedding dress and have time for some other things."

"Other things sound fun," Riley shook her tits at Nick not minding that an approaching salesman could clearly see her exposure. She put the straps on her shoulders ignoring the man's stare.

"Mr. Nicholas, great to see you. I hope everything is going well with the car?" the salesman shook Nick's hand. "And who is this gorgeous lady that you have with you?"

"This is my fiance' Riley," Nick said.

The salesman looked into Riley's eyes as if she was a goddess. "What can I interest you in today?"

"Same make, model and features, but in champagne pink," Nick said.

"I have a pink peril," the salesman said.

"We'll take it," Riley snapped.

Nicholas laughed.

"I'll go get the keys and get started on the paperwork," the salesman smiled.

"I'm looking for a better deal on this one," Nick called after him.

The salesman waved hurrying off to the show room.

"I almost forgot that you are decedent from the aristocracy," Riley chuckled taking hold of his arm.

"Comes in handy at times like these though, huh?" Nicholas laughed.

"If we got married, would that make me a gold-digger?" Riley said.

"Maybe," Nick joked.

"I hope not," Riley said sincerely.

"I was just joking," Nick said.

The sports convertible was brought out and Riley got in the driver's seat. She loved the white leather seats and knew that Shana would love it.

"All I need is your signatures sir," the salesman presented the paperwork to Nicholas.

Nick signed the papers glancing over at Riley sitting in the drivers seat of the car. He had known her most of his life and she seemed to look more beautiful every time he looked at her.

"Take me somewhere and fuck me," Riley said getting out of the car. "I think you and I should get married."

****

"Are you sure you want to do this?" Shana gasped trying to catch her breath holding her knees up to her shoulders.

Rico rubbed the head of his hard cock over her wet pussy. "I know its strange with everything going so fast, but you've seen it for yourself. Riley and Nick are much better together and we really get each other," he said pressing his dick slowly into Shana's vagina. "We're all going to still be together. I think this is why Riley suggested this, so we can see for ourselves."

"Maybe," Shana moaned. She knew that he would reason anything to justify filling her with his big dick. Any excuse would do. She hooked her heels behind his thighs rolling her hips against his grind.

****

"I love this place!" Riley squealed striping out of her jumpsuit and running naked out on the sand. She didn't stop until the waves knocked her down.

"You are so amazing!" Nick laugh swooping her up in his arms.

"And you are so handsome and exciting," Riley laughed kissing him again and again. "I wanted to fuck on this beach for a long time."

"You don't mind strangers watching?" Nick said sitting her down on the edge letting the waves splash over them.

"You like people watching you too, don't you," Riley giggled.

"It's the thrill," Nick said turning her over on her knees.

Some nudist stopped to watch and others only paused for a moment. They drew a pretty good crowd of thirty or so. Some of the men stroked their cocks.

Riley screamed out her pleasures thrusting her ass back as fast and hard as Nick pounded her asshole.

Nicholas strained his muscles ensuring that his veins swelled. Mostly for show, but he was giving Riley everything that he had. Their climax was even bigger. Riley screamed and Nicholas grunted. He pulled out his dick shooting streams of cum clear over her head and on her back. Nick pulled Riley back into the water to the cheers and applause of the crowd.

Riley laughed hysterically in Nick's arms. "Yes! I love people watching," she kissed him wildly. "I know you want my pussy and I want to give it to you, but can we please wait until our wedding?"

"I want you a virgin," Nicholas said lifting her up again and carrying her out of the water. "We still have some shopping to do."

"I bet that Rico getting Shana's pussy," Riley chuckled.

"Why do you say that?" Nick asked.

"Because I have to hold Rico off and Shana is not going to resist him," she giggled.

"You planned all of this, didn't you?" Nick said holding her hand as they walked by to his SUV.

"Not all of it," Riley laughed. "As soon as y'all brought up about fucking me and Shana, I could tell Rico was dying to fuck Shana. I just gave them a reason to get together, and I wanted to know for sure that you wanted to do more than fuck me. I had a feeling you did. I just wanted to be sure. Spoiler alert! If they are fucking like I think they are, they are going to be willing to switch wedding partners."

"I had my suspicions," Nick said. "I just wanted to be with you. We just seem to have more fun together." He opened the back of his vehicle. "I really don't mind marrying Shana. It makes since with keeping us all together. It's a lot less complicated me marrying you instead of Shana. We are actually first cousins, my mom's brother is her dad, but he didn't marry her mother."

"I'm just thinking about being your wife," Riley giggled. "You are fucking my mother."

"Are you thinking about a threesome?" Nicholas joked.

Riley laughed hysterically.

"You can play in that cute little box you came in," he teased.

"I'm pretty sure Becky would love to have you dick her down," Riley replied. "She seemed to be in favor of you and I getting married."

"She did say that Rico and Shana are better suited for each other," Nick chuckled. He took her full tits in his hands. "Sometimes I can't get over how gorgeous you are."

"That means a lot coming from the hottest guy in this town," Riley said kissing him and stroking his cock. "We better go before this thing finds its way back up my ass."

"We should go by that store Bohemian Boutique," he said getting back in his clothes. "Shana hustled up some good deals there."

"She got an entire wardrobe for she and I there," Riley said strapping back on her wedged sandals.

"Let's do the same for her and Rico. He could use a bit of a makeover," Nick chuckled.

Riley giggled.

They picked up Shana's wedding dress from the bridle boutique, had boiled Cajun crawfish with lobster, shrimp, corn and potatoes, and then went to the jewelry store.

"Nice to see you again," the salesman behind the jewelry counter greeted Nicholas as he entered with Riley.

"This one," Riley said having an eye for fine jewelry. "She didn't own many herself, but she was fascinated by them. "Shana loves pink. It will be perfect for her. Size six."

"You heard the lady," Nicholas said putting his credit card on the counter.

"Yes sir," the salesman said.

"I like this ban for you," Riley said. "I like that tribal design and the thickest gold."

"Box it up," Nick told the salesman.

Riley put her arm around Nick's waist then squeezed his ass firmly.

"Y'all make such an adorable couple," an older lady who was browsing the store complimented them.

"I know, and he is so lean and fine," Riley smiled running her hand over Nick's chest. "And he has a really big cock too," she added in a whisper to the old woman.

The old woman blushed and giggled moving down the counter.

Nick chuckled putting his arm around Riley then sliding his hand down over her buttcheeks.

"Here you go sir," the salesmen returned. "Insured twice the purchase price to reflect market changes."

"Remember her," Nicholas said to the salesmen. "She loves fine jewelry."

Riley leaned over in Nick's lap and began sucking his cock as he drove them to the Bohemian Boutique. It was a good sunny day for shopping with lots of smiling people about. Nicholas loved the scene with lots of street vendors peddling their wears on carts. Riley stopped and smelled the flowers. One smile spread from person to person.

"Hello," the clerk in the Bohemian Boutique greeted Nicholas and Riley when the entered the store.

"Hello," Riley smiled.

"Can I pick out a few things for you?" Nick asked looking at one of the dressed mannequins.

Riley blushed and giggled.

Nicholas began pulling items off the racks. Riley tried on several of the items she favored but did not decline any of the things that Nick selected. Nick piled so many clothes on the counter that the sales girls got separate racks to hold them. Riley laughed at how Nick playful selected a sample of just about everything they had in the store.

"We're going to need a car to deliver all of this home," Nick said.

"We have a delivery van sir," the sales woman smiled brightly ringing up the purchases item by item.

"We need to get Shana's car into the garage without her seeing it also," Nick added.

"If she's at home, I'll just keep her busy while you park the car in the garage," Riley said. "We're going to have to store all of these things in the garage also."

They loaded up the store's delivery van driven by one of the sales clerks. Riley drove Shana's new car from the dealership and they caravan home. As their luck held, Rico's car was not in the driveway. They got the new car and all of the clothes and accessories into the garage quickly.

"This is so much fun and we have plenty of daylight left," Riley said falling into Nick's arms.

"What would you like to do next?" Nick asked kissing her neck and groping tits.

"I'm thinking of you putting this thing in me," she giggled rubbing his hardon.

"Sounds great to me," Nick chuckled swooping her up in his arms and carrying her off to the master bedroom.

CHAPTER FIVE

Riley burst through the front door just ahead of Nick having won the race on the last half block of their morning run. She laughed cheering her victory. She and Nick had jogged to the gym, had a good workout and jogged home. She got a good head start on the race sprinting ahead of him and cutting him off leaping over their white picked fence.

"Good morning. Looks like y'all had a good workout this morning," Shana said cooking breakfast along side Rico in the kitchen.

"It was great!" Riley giggled giving Shana and Rico a kiss on their cheeks.

"She's a beast doing squats," Nick said getting bottle waters from the frig. "My thighs are burning."

"That's how she got that amazing ass," Shana swatted Riley's buttcheeks with an open palm.

"I wasn't born with great genetics and a wonderful degree of melanin, so I have to work harder at it," Riley replied.

Rico, Shana and Nicholas laughed.

"Babe, you are the epitome of the world's view of beauty," Nicholas said. "long blonde hair, incestuous blue eyes, symmetrically sharp facial features, plump high lifted breasts, curvy hips and shapely legs. You are what most of the world strive to be."

"I was thinking of coloring me hair red," Riley replied to the others amusement.

"You are perfect the way you are, but I will support whatever you decide to do," Nick said pulling her into his sweaty arms.

"We're having breakfast out back," Shana interrupted.

"It smells great," Riley said still looking into Nick's deep brown eyes. "We'll clean up and meet you guys out there." She kissed his lips and pulled him away.

"We need to tell them," Shana said.

"Yea, I agree," Rico nodded finishing the orange juice.

Rico and Shana laid out the breakfast platters on the picnic table in the backyard with fresh fruits. Nicholas and Riley joined them shortly.

"You two look really good together," Nick said tossing Rico the engagement ring in a black box that Riley selected. "I think that's better than my pinky ring."

Riley snuggled up closer to Nick watching as Rico got up from his seat to knee in front of Shana.

"Wow, I get to do this twice," Rico mused. "I didn't see this coming, but over the past couple of days its come clear. Riley and I have been together forever it seems, but you have been there also. I've confessed my desires for you to Riley many times as she has spoke of her feelings for Nick. We are all best friends, and nothing will change that. This is to solidify my special bond with you. Will you marry me?"

Nick and Riley held each other in joyful hope.

"Yes," Shana exhaled. "Yes, I will marry you."

Riley cheered loudly. "I knew it would workout," she gleamed. "I'm even happier now. This is so perfect."

"Looks like I'm handing the cherry over to you bro," Rico chuckled.

"I am honored to receive it," Nick laughed.

"I hate spoiling a surprise," Riley said to everyone's amusement. She looked at Nick pulling on his arm to get up from the table.

Shana and Rico watched as Nick and Riley went over to the garage. They opened the doors revealing not one, but two European convertible sport cars and racks of clothes.

"Oh my stars!" Shana exclaimed running over to hug Riley.

"You did it for me, so I just had to do it for you," Riley kissed her best friend's cheek.

"Hey bro, there's a rack over here for you too," Nick chuckled.

"Man you're ballin'," Rico hugged Nick. "Thank you my brother."

"I know you'd take care of me too," Nick replied.

"Nick picked out the clothes for us," Riley confessed.

"He has great taste," Shana replied looking through the racks of clothes.

"I hate to kiss and run, but Riley and I have some house calls to make," Nick said pulling Riley away. "Don't wait up for us."

"What do you have up your sleeves?" Riley giggled following Nick back into the house.

"We need to visit our mothers again. This news will come to great relief to them," he said getting his keys.

"Should I change?" Riley giggled flipping up her short floral dress showing him her perfectly naked body.

"Absolutely not. That is a gorgeous outfit," Nick chuckled.

Riley slipped on her sandals and grabbed her bag. She dangled a few pieces of jewelry around her neck and wrists adding just the right amount of styling to her liking.

Riley worked Nick's cock out of his pants as soon as he backed out of their driveway. She stroked it slowly mesmerized by its length and girth.

"That really did go a lot easier than I had imagined," Nick said leaning back more in his seat.

"I imagined that it was easier than confessing that he had fucked her pussy," Riley said. "I'm relieved also, otherwise I would have had to tell Rico that I wanted to marry you instead of him."

"I can see that going badly in many different ways," Nick replied.

"I'm glad that they were able to see the same thing as we have," Riley said.

"You are ready to break loose and I can imagine that Rico wouldn't be able to handle that," Nick said.

"Yea, they are more closet freaks. You and I are open with our sexuality," Riley said leaning over taking the head of Nick's huge cock in her mouth.

Nick combed his fingers through her long thick curls brushing it away to reveal her painted cock sucking lips. "Oh fuck!" he groaned straining to maintain the vehicle on the road. The tingling sensation of his approach climax started to engulf him. He got the vehicle over to the shoulder of the road and in park just before the first stream shot into Riley's greedy mouth. "Shit! Shit! Fuck!" he exclaimed with each burst of his thick seed exploded from the head of his big black dick.

He gripped a handful of her hair thrusting his cock into her throat shimmering as another volley of sperm. Riley guzzled as if she was drinking from a jug.

"Oh fuck! Nick strained pressing his feet against the floor board. "Fuck, I'm dizzy."

Riley giggled wiping the corners of her mouth with her finger. "That was like a cup full," she laughed.

"I see why people smoke after sex," Nick chuckled trying to calm his breathing. "It was like a knockout punch to the head."

"Your nut is fast becoming my addiction," she mused. "We should freeze it and my eggs, so we'll have some left for when we want to have children."

Nick laughed finally able to stuff his cock back in his pants. He knew that the prospect of Riley allowing herself to get fat was unthinkable. He pulled the SUV back out on the road.

"I like the way you handle me, pulling my hair and fucking my face," Riley said checking out her makeup. "I feel really safe with you."

"I'm glad about that," Nick replied. "Because I think we're about to do some really crazy shit."

"I'm down," Riley giggled.

It took them another ten minutes to get to Riley's mother's house. The vintage home was surrounded by a ten foot stone wall covered in ivy. Riley opened the gate locking it back as it was one of Rachel's long standing rules. The gate is locked for a reason, so leave it as you find it.

Rachel's backyard garden featured a platform pallet framed bed with a variety of large pillows, a rock waterfall koi pond, a fire pit, a couple of chase lounges, and a bamboo wet bar all in brilliant colors and filled with medicinal plants, herbs and spices. Rachel was reading curled on one of the chased lounges when Nick and Riley made their way through the grape vine path.

"Riley, Nick I was just thinking about you two. Please join me," Rachel greeted them with hugs and kisses.

"We have some more news," Riley said taking her mother's arm and sitting down with her.

Rachel returned their smiles eager to hear what they had to share.

"We realized that Rico and Shana are a better match," Riley began as Nick made them screw driver cocktails with slices of orange at the wet bar. "You and Becky made some very good points. The good news is that Shana and Rico came to the same conclusion. The wedding will go on as planned but Nick and I will marry and Shana and Rico will get hitched."

"I'm sure Becky loved hearing this," Rachel hugged her daughter.

"We haven't told her yet," Nick said handing them the orange juice and vodka cocktails.

"I love the way Nick is and I don't want nothing to change for him except for adding me to his lifestyle," Riley said blowing Nick a kiss. "I've always admired the way women drool over him and how generous he is with them, especially with you. I don't want anything to change between the two of you, if anything I want it to grow. I know that he will support me as well."

"I definitely will," Nick replied. "I love watching you do it as much as I like doing it with you."

"I was thinking that when she gets ready for us to have her some grandchildren she can carry them for us," Riley said.

"Riley!" Rachel exclaimed.

"Or my mom," Nick added.

"Nicholas!" Rachel held her hand up to bring a halt to that line of thinking.

"At any rate, you said that you enjoyed having sex with my mother and I want you to continue," Riley said.

"Hello, sitting right here," Rachel interrupted. "First of all, its your choice if or when you decided you want children. Being pregnant with you shut down this baby making machine permanently. I didn't know that Nick was interested in being in a relationship with you or anyone when we hooked up. I'm not going to have sex with my daughter's husband."

Riley giggled.

"What?" Rachel replied.

"You raised me to be open to new possibilities," Riley chuckled as Nick approached them.

Nick took Rachel's hand and pulled her to her feet. She put up no resistance to him smashing his firm body against hers. Rachel gasped just before he crushed his lips against hers.

Riley curled her legs up on the chase lounge watching Nick walk her mother over to the garden bed. She giggled seeing the book her mother had been reading was a romance novel.

Nicholas worked his tongue against Rachel's tongue while unbuttoning her maxi dress to reveal her large swollen tits. He squeezed the heavy melons, sucking on one of the erect nipples then the other.

"Oh! Oh!" Rachel moaned stepping out the dress.

Nick laid her back on the thick mattress kissing and licking his way down to her aching clit. He attacked it wildly shaking his head with the bud clamped between his lips.

Rachel held his head in place grinding against his face. She found herself back where they had left off. Her orgasm built quickly then released. She moaned loader feeling the sparks of another climax.

Nick quickly stripped out of his clothes mounting her. He held her knees up pumping his big black dick balls deep inside her thirsty cunt.

"Oh fuck!" Rachel cried out another climax. She held his arms tight as he pounded her relentlessly. She was cumming so hard, one orgasm after another. She thrust her hips up to meet his powerful strokes.

Nick flipped her over bringing her ass up to give him a straight shot to the depths of her womanhood. He grunted pulling her back as he slammed into her with all his might. Every stroke seemed to make his cock harder.

"Yes! Please!" Rachel cried out.

Riley glanced up from the book and smiled. She could see the future. Undoubtedly her hips would get wider and her boobs larger. She was a spitting image of her mother. Seeing Nick devour Rachel's mature curves assured that he would still find her attractive when she got older. She enjoyed the right now, but was always planning for the future.

Nick flipped Rachel over again putting her legs on his shoulders as he drilled her hot pussy. "Oh yeah, I love this good stuff," he grunted pumping his dick faster.

Rachel's eyes rolled back in her head. She had gone past all of her experiences. His cock was just the right size to stuff her full and hit the right spots. Her entire body trembled. She was slipping further and further away.

"Ugh!" Nick grunted flooding Rachel's hot cunt with his thick jism.

"Bring that stick over here, so I can clean it up," Riley mused. She had tasted Shana, but the very thought of tasting her mother excited her more.

Rachel held herself tight basking in the glow of the incredible sex she had just experienced. The first time made her want more, but the promise of getting it on a regular made it more special.

Riley licked and sucked Nick's cock and balls clean of his cum and her mother's juices. She could tell the difference with her mother's cream mixed with his. "It tastes as good as it looked," she giggled.

"Shit! I never thought I'd want to get married, now I can hardly wait," Nick chuckled gathering his clothes allowing time to herself.

"You're ready to pop my cherry, huh?" Riley laughed.

"Hell yeah!" Nick replied. "I'm thinking that yours is going to be as good as hers. I don't know how I'm going to have the time to fuck anybody else." He kissed her and sat down next to her with a fresh cocktail.

Riley laughed snuggling up next to him on the chase lounger.

CHAPTER SIX

"Are you okay?" Shana asked seeing Rico appearing to struggle to get off the bed.

"I was just thinking that I might not have another nut in me," he chuckled stumbling to his feet.

"You know, I was kinda hoping that it turned out like this a long time ago," Shana said turning on the shower. "I use to skip out, so that Riley wouldn't see how much I wanted to be with you."

"Funny, she use to call you my girlfriend when no one else was around because she has caught me staring at you," Rico smiled.

"I try to be as open and honest as Riley, but I have too many secrets," Shana said.

"You mean like fucking Mr. Jordan Fallon?" Rico said. "That was easy to see as much money as he dropped on you and for Riley. Nick and I picked up that right away."

"Are you cool with that?" Shana asked.

"I've thought about you fucking some of the guys you went out with, but nothing was as exciting as watching you do it with Nick," Rico said. "I don't want you to change. I just want to be apart of it."

"Are you okay with me spending time with Mr. Jordan?" Shana asked washing his chest.

"Do you mind me knowing and telling me about it?" Rico asked.

"I don't want it to be a problem," Shana said.

"As long as you tell me what's up, I'm going to be down with you," Rico said.

"Then, Mr. Jordan wants to see me today," Shana said.

"When?" he asked.

"About an hour," Shana said stroking his cock. "He's going to want me to give him some."

"Do you give him head?" Rico asked.

"How much do you want to know?" Shana asked.

"Everything," he replied.

"Yes, I give him head and we do everything including anal," Shana said. "He's about your size and has lots of stamina."

"Do you like it?" Rico asked.

"Yes, he's real good at it," Shana said stroking his cock faster. She cupped his balls and within a minute he was shooting his cum against her belly.

"You think I'm weird, huh? Liking the idea of you fucking other guys" Rico asked as they got out of the shower.

"No, it turns me on that you like watching me and knowing about me with other guys. It makes me feel totally free," Shana said drying off. "I'd like for you to do stuff too. There's a bunch of girls that like you. Riley told me about some and I have seen others checking you out. You could have had as many girls as Nick if you wasn't with Riley. All I say is no other girls in our bed other than Riley."

"Deal," Rico chuckled. "How about the Gypsies?"

"Sure," Shana smiled figuring Nicholas must have told him about his playtime with the older women. "Which one do you like best?"

"I like all of them, but I was thinking about Willow," Rico said.

"I like her," Shana said putting on a floral patterned button up mini sundress. "If she's not home then Mrs. Marie. She's always pushing her big boobs in people faces."

"I've seen them. They popped out over at Nick's house. They are really nice," Rico chuckled.

"Shit, I'm going to be late," Shana said putting on her white sneakers.

"I'll get your clothes in from the garage," Rico said following her out to move his car to let her out of the garage. He smiled at how hot Shana looked with her sunglasses and the drop top down on the convertible. He realized that he hadn't thought much about Riley at all. He knew that she was safe with Nick and could let loose some of her inhibitions he could see her holding back with him. His mind went to Willow and Mrs. Marie as he began bringing the racks of clothes into the house. He had never gone after a girl before. He and Riley had just been thrown together because of their friendship. Nothing was ever decided about them dating. More than anything, they were friends.

Rico put on one of the new linen outfits Nick had picked out for him, way more dressy than his normal wears. He did, however, like the new sandals. It was a look he felt he could get use to.

His cock was rock hard in the fine material thinking about holding Willow's shapely body in his arms. He could see her light brown eyes staring back at him in his mind, and her bright smile. He would fuck her the way Riley had always demanded and how Shana enjoyed it. He would suck on her clit and finger her pussy.

Before Rico realized it, he was parked in Willow's driveway. Her rugged jeep was parked in front of him with the top off.

"This is a wonderful surprise," Willow greeted Rico coming out of her house. She was barefoot wearing a long skirt and a thin top that did very little to hide her big braless tits. She hugged him tight smashing her big tits against his young firm chest.

"I've never visited you here before. I have my mind set on you," Rico smiled trying to be bold to hide his nervousness.

"Really? And without your partner Nicholas, I see," Willow batted her long eye lashes at him. "Let's go inside so you can show me what's on your mind."

Rico followed Willow inside the house with his eyes glued to the movements of her asscheeks under her skirt. His unrestrained hardon pushed out the front on his linen pants.

"I understand that you are a virgin," Willow said pouring them both a glass of wine.

"Not anymore," Rico said. He did not see her unbutton her top. It laid open hooked on her dark brown erect nipples. "I'm with Shana now. We are going to have a double wedding on Saturday. Nick is going to marry Riley and I am going to marry Shana."

"That definitely makes more sense," Willow said handing Rico the big wine glass and then removing her top. "I've always felt that you and Riley were more of the brother and sister type. I can definitely see you and Shana as a better match. I didn't foresee Nicholas getting marry, however he and Riley make a more perfect union. I see that you came here to have sex with me." She rubbed her hand over his hardon while loosing her skirt. She dropped her skirt and pulled out his cock.

Rico took both of the huge tits in his hands squeezing them firmly and rubbing his thumbs over the hard nipples. "These are wonderful," he continued massaging them.

"Mmmm, your hands feels good," Willow moaned. She stroked his cock and handled his ballsack enjoying the pleasure of her breasts being fondled.

Rico kissed her lips softly then again and again continuing to play with the large melons.

"Mmmm, let me suck your dick," Willow moaned as she knelt. She twisted up and down his shaft with both hands stacked on top of one another licking and sucking on the circumcised head.

He put his hand on her head thrusting his cock to her throat. His sexual experience had been limited to Riley and Shana. The ease in-which Willow took his entire length into her mouth let him know that he still had a lot to learn.

Willow smashed her face against his pelvis beckoning for more cock to slid down her throat. "You like having your dick sucked, don't you," she mused.

Rico groaned rocking his hips back and forth in her grip. Looking up at him, she appeared to be younger with his nutsack in her mouth.

"Let's get you comfortable," Willow stood helping him out of his shirt. "All of the fine ones stick together." She scratched her manicured fingernails over his chest and rippling stomach muscles.

Rico's hands went right back to her brown swollen melons. Shana's breasts were still getting bigger and he imagined one day that hers would be as voluptuous.

Willow laid Rico down on the large floor pillows and took up his big black cock again. She licked up and down his shaft sucking on his balls and the head of his dick. "You handsome boy," she moaned straddling his hips. She guided the fat circumcised head into her hot pussy easing all the way down the shaft.

Rico squeezed the large beautiful tits sucking hard on one of the erect nipples then the other while Willow bucked and rolled her hips on the young man's monster cock. She screamed out her pleasures getting all that she could from the huge cock inside of her.

****

"You have a different glow about you," Jordan said looking Shana up and down. "I think married life is going to be fitting for you."

"It's working out real good," Shana smiled. "I'm going to marry Rico on Saturday. I feel really happy about it."

"It shows," Jordan replied. "You are smiling and your skin is glowing." He lifted her short dress taking a peek at her smooth brown pussy. "Delicious."

"What do you think of my wedding present?" Shana said striking a pose against her new sports car.

"It fits you. Let me guess, Nicholas?" he smiled.

"Naturally, he always give the kinds of gifts that elevates you. You are doing the same. Thank you again for the wardrobe," Shana replied.

"Spending time with you is more than thanks enough," Jordan said taking her hand. "It's getting close to your wedding date so I'm assuming that you don't have very much time to spare. How can I help you?"

"Nicholas is always so generous, I'd like to give them a gift that matches his sentiment," she said leaning into him.

"What does he like?" Jordan asked smoothing his hand over her round asscheeks.

"He only talks about making money and having sex. He has Riley now, so he is very satisfied. I was thinking about some kind of investment opportunity that he could make money on," Shana replied rubbing his hardon through his pants.

"I think I might have something that could be a very good investment," Jordan said sliding his hands under Shana's dress squeezing her beautiful brown ass. "If you don't mind taking a drive with me?"

"I'll drive," Shana said giving him a kiss.

They drove to an abandoned bay front motel that had a mile long throughway from the main road. It had covered picnic benches along the beach. Fifty rooms were spanned equally from the lobby with a pool and botanical garden. A pier with a privacy fence blocked in the private swimming area.

"This is all private property from the main road out beyond the pier. This could make an ideal private resort for naturalists like yourselves and nudist. An oasis. The nude beaches in the area are small with no amenities. Look around at the possibilities. I picked it up from a bank for a steal, five hundred thousand," Jordan said taking his shoes off to walk on the sand. "With a little spit and polish this place could be a gold mind."

Shana walked around imagining people sun bathing around the pool, nudists walking along the beach, gatherings at the picnic areas and swimmers splashing in the water. She removed her sandals and walked to one of the covered picnic tables. She sat on top of the table and removed her dress letting the warm breeze from the bay blanket her smooth brown skin.

Jordan walked along the waters edge imagining having a young beauty of his on, holding hands and kissing at sunset. Shana had sparked those possibilities in him. He was reaching the age of retirement and he wanted a single joy in his life, to renounce his bachelorhood, to be with only one true love.

Shana was laid back on the picnic table basking in the peaceful joy of the place when Jordan approached.

"So what do you think?" Jordan asked.

"I love it," Shana said leaning up on her elbows. "How would this work? What terms would you want, because its a lot of money you are talking about."

"I want you to set me up with a young beautiful naturalist like you," Jordan smiled. "I want a young wife."

Shana had the same thoughts when Nicholas asked to marry her. Jordan was a bachelor who didn't even allow visitors into his home as it was with Nicholas who had never taken a girl on a single date. She didn't see herself as a married woman, but she was never opposed to relationships. Jordan was obviously wealthy and could buy just about any woman of his choosing. Why the change of heart though it didn't matter much. "What are you looking for? What kind of woman?" she asked.

"Tall, slim, nice boobs and butt with a naturalist open mind," Jordan said. "The rest would have to be chemistry between the two of us."

"White, black, brown, Asian?" she asked.

"It doesn't matter. I never had a preference to race," he replied. "Look for someone like you."

Shana thought of all the girls that she knew that were open minded enough to consider Jordan in a serious relationship. Seven of them came to mind. She would have to speak to them to find out where their hearts lay. "Okay," she said. "I will setup some meetings for you."

"Fabulous!" Jordan said giving her a kiss on the forehead then walking back to the waters edge.

CHAPTER EIGHT

St. Anne street was lined with cars in both directions before sunrise. The neighbors had been gracious and most of them were in attendance to the spiritual event. It was an all white affair from the bride and groom to the caters and flowers. White lace and silk dress were worn in a variety of styles.

A joyful tune whistled from a pair of flute players just as the sun broke through the trees shinning down on the wedding party. Riley and Shana walked slowly over the rice paper to the alter where their grooms stood proudly.

It was standing room only, but no one minded being shoulder to shoulder and front to back to witness the joyous occasion. Some of the guess wrapped their arms around the waist of others they had not formally met. Love was like a blanket comforting the souls.

When the grooms embraced and kissed their brides, so did the guests exchanged kisses among themselves. Husbands kissing their bridges, boyfriends kissing their girlfriends, wives kissing men and husbands kissing women and even the caterers shared kisses with some of the guests.

The Gypsies where the first in line to kiss the brides and grooms. The other guests took their turns giving passionate kisses, men and women kissing the brides and women kissing the grooms. The brides and grooms thanked each and everyone for their guests, taking pictures and sharing laughs and smiles.

"I want you right now," Riley whispered to her husband, Nicholas.

"Where?" Nick whispered back holding her close to him.

"The attic," Riley said pulling him away.

They gave more thanks to the guests as they made their way into the house and up the winding stairs to the attic.

"Hurry!" Riley urged wiggling out of her wedding dress. "I've been waiting years for this and I don't want to wait one second more. We will have lots of time later, but right now I want you to pop this cherry."

"You got it wifey," Nick chuckled laying Riley back on the ottoman.

Riley held her knees up and spread wide so that she watch her husband burst through her gates. Nick positioned himself, placing the head of his big rock hard cock to her vagina opening. He had deflowered many virgins before, but with them he took his time. Riley didn't want that. He held his big rod steady and with one hard thrust he tore through her hymen. He kept pumping his cock hard and deep trying to more her pain to pleasure. It worked. The grimace on Riley's face fell as an orgasm took over the pain.

Riley cried out her pleasure and pain through joyous tears and laughter. She begged for more humping up against his powerful thrusts. Her passion filled the attic and spread through the joists and walls.

"Sounds like Nicholas and Riley are getting their honeymoon started," Jordan muse walking up behind Rico and Shana with Dani on his arm.

"Jordan, Dani," Shana turned with a bright smile. Dani was one of the girls she knew that would possibly be interested in Jordan. She was a stunning beautiful light brown skinned girl who grew up without a father figure in her life. She was also a virgin just graduating from Catholic school with no street knowledge. "I didn't see you guys earlier." She kissed Jordan firmly on the lips.

"We had some business at the court house to take care of this morning," Jordan said holding up Dani's left hand to show off her wedding set.

Rico and Dani stared into each others eyes without saying a word.

"Wow! You really work fast, don't you? What happened to your decree of bachelorship?" Shana mused.

"She changed my mind as soon as I say her," Jordan laughed happily.

Rico studied the light brown color of Dani's eyes, the shape of her nose, the pink gloss of her full lips, the even light brown tone of skin, and the fullness of her swollen tits displayed in the deep-V lace gown that allowed her light brown areola and nipples to show through.

"Kiss her already," Shana nudged Rico.

Rico pulled her firmly against his body moving his eyes from hers to her lips and into her eyes again. Dani wrapped her long slender arms around his neck melting into his kiss. Their mouths opened and closed sucking at each others tongues.

"Anyways," Jordan turned his attention back to Shana. "I don't know if y'all have any honeymoon plans, but I'd like to bestow a honeymoon to Tahiti on Nicholas and Riley in exchange for a double honeymoon with you and Rico at Blackish Island Resort. It doesn't look like they will have and objections."

Shana chuckled as Rico and Dani continued making out. "When would we leave?" she asked.

"Right away, but the tickets to Tahiti are for tomorrow," Jordan said looking up at the ceiling hearing Riley's cries of pleasure.

"Let's do it," Shana said. She changed out of her wedding dress into a spaghetti strapped mini sundress and helped Rico pack a few things for them. She took the honeymoon reservations to Becky and Rachel for Nick and Riley, and only told them that she and Rico were heading off to their own honeymoon. She avoided mentioning Jordan to her Aunt Becky. They were whisked away in a town car with Jordan and Dani already inside.

"Champagne?" Jordan said popping the cork on the bottle. "To bohemian beauty," he toasted.

"Naturalist beauty," Rico countered pulling gently on Dani's natural soft curls.

"Yes, natural beauties," Jordan agreed kissing Shana softly.

The helicopter ride to the private island resort took a mere half hour, and Shana, Rico, Jordan and Dani were settled into their combined bungalow before sunset.

"I'd like to spend some time getting to know Dani a little better if that's okay with you two?" Rico asked.

"Ah sure," Shana shrugged her shoulders.

"That's great," Jordan replied. "Up for a nude stroll along the beach?"

"I'd love to," Shana said tossing her towel on a chair and began removing her bikini.

Dani was back in Rico's arms. Neither of them heard the rest of what Jordan and Shana had to say before they left.

"Why hadn't I seen you before?" Rico asked breaking their kiss.

"I went to Catholic school and my mother required that I keep myself covered," Dani said. "I've seen you many times with Shana, your girlfriend Riley and Nicholas. Y'all come to my mother's store often on St. Paul street. I usually stay in the back."

Rico could not place her.

"I met Shana walking by my school and we talked a few times, that's how I know her," Dani added. "Shana introduced me to Jordan yesterday and he completely changed my entire world in hours, but I never could have imagined being this close to you in this way." She kissed him hungrily.

Rico walked Dani over to the bed stripping away what was left of their clothes. He spread her legs wide attacking her clit, pussy and anus. Dani squeezed her own tits and nipples moaning out her pleasures. She raised her heels flexing her calves and trembling thigh muscles to Rico's delight.

"Yes! Yes! Yes!" Dani exclaimed her climax. She bucked and grind holding his head in place. Of all the wonders Jordan had told her about, he had yet to put his hands on her. She believed that it would be Jordan instead of Rico who would take her virginity. "Rico. Rico, I'm a virgin," she warned.

Rico popped his head up. Her eyes looked golden in the last bit of daylight shining through the window curtains.

"I'm a virgin," she repeated.

Rico climbed over her. His chest swelled with joy. "We will go slow," he whispered kissing her passionately. He swollen dickhead found its mark. He pushed steadily breaking through the gates to her womanhood.

Dani strained holding on to him tightly. The pain wasn't near as harsh as she imagined. She rolled her hips back against him feeling the strangeness of having someone inside of her for the first time. She had kissed and made out with boys and girls, but had never gone further than giving blowjobs at school.

Rico pumped his cock steadily increasing the rhythm gradually until he was pounding her with abandon. Memories of Riley professing how she wanted him to fuck her until she was unconscious on their wedding night flooded his mind. He was not with Riley. Dani felt different, special in a way that he could not describe. He could feel how she wanted him to give it to her and she responded to every stroke he delivered.

Dani wrapped her kneels around the backs of Rico's thighs giving herself more leverage to thrust her hips up to meet him. She could feel another orgasm rising. She moaned and strained pulling his hips down guiding his strokes. It was everything that she never knew she wanted or desired. Her body trembled. She squeezed him holding him in place as the rode the waves of her orgasm.

"Are you okay?" Rico asked once she loosened her death grip on him.

"Better than okay," she smiled up at him. "But I'm starving."

"Let's go see what we can find," Rico said slowing sliding his still rock hard cock from her freshly deflowered pussy. He looked down at her caught again in her gorgeous eyes. He pulled her to her feet and kissed her passionately again. "I can't keep my hands off of you."

"We can shower each other," she smiled allowing him to continue to hold her tight. Her pussy throbbed and with his hardon pressed against her stomach, she wouldn't have objected if he laid her back down in spite of the growling stomach.

"As beautiful as you are, I love it even more that you are natural," Rico said walking her to the shower.

"I had not choice really," Dani replied. "I was never allowed to wear makeup. I'm not opposed to a little makeup, but I am not a fan of weaves or extensions."

"You don't need any of those things," Rico said pulling her into the shower. "Your skin is flawless and your hair is soft. I really love these too." He lifted her heavy boobs.

"I'm glad I don't have to keep them wrapped and covered up anymore. My mother is upset now, but she will get over it," she said gingerly taking hold of Rico's rigid cock. She stroked it slowly and massaged his nutsack. "I really like your dick too."

"How did Mr. Jordan get a hold of you?" Rico said soaping up Dani's big jugs.

"Shana came to me and told me that she wanted to introduce me to a man who could get me out of my depression," Dani said washing his back. "He took me shopping and I tried on all these different clothes. The more I tried on, the better I felt. I felt in control of my own life. The dresses were so pretty. He told me that if I married him that I wouldn't have to live by anyone else's rules but my own. We spent the night on the beach by a fire and this morning we went to the court house and got married. He proved his point when you looked at me at the wedding. I wanted you more than I ever wanted anything in my life, now here we are."

Rico kissed her passionately again crushing her breast between them. He wanted to take her back to bed, but he knew she was as hungry as he.

Dani wrapped herself in a white floral pattern sarong matching her white painted finger and toe nails. She done her wrists and ankles with an assortment of white beads, shells and charms similar to the ones Riley and Shana usually wore.

She loved the way Rico looked at her as they walk across the white sand. His eyes smiled brighter than his lips. She leaned against him as they made their way to the buffet comforted by his strong arms around her. Everything felt right. She was honestly happy for the first time in her young life.

"Yeah you two," Jordan called out to them from his seat at the buffet table next to Shana. "Come join us."

Some people wore swimwear, some wore clothes but most of the people around the circular buffet table were nude like Jordan and Shana.

"I'm surprised y'all made it out of the room," Shana mused sitting Dani down next to her.

"I'm just so hungry," Dani replied reaching out to take a roasted chicken leg from the platter in front of her. "Thank y'all so much. I have never been this happy in my life. Can I stay with Rico, like when we get back?"

"Of course, if that's what you want," Jordan chuckled.

"Rico we were talking about that," Shana said. "It's obvious that y'all want to be together, so Dani should move in with us. Jordan and I already have an arrangement. We would only be adding one more natural beauty to our love nest."